3/20/82

Hefter

Munch

| DATE DUE | | |
|---|---|---|
| MAY 8 1982 | JAN. 26 1985 | OCT. 22 1987 |
| JUN. 29 | MAR. 16 1985 | AUG. 26 1989 |
| FEB. 19 1983 | AUG. 15 1985 | NOV. 23 1992 |
| MAR. 26 1983 | MAR. 8 1986 | AUG. 09 1993 |
| MAY 7 1983 | MAR. 24 1986 | OCT. 02 1993 |
| MAY 28 1983 | JUN. 28 1986 | JUN 17 1999 |
| AUG. 22 1983 | SEP. 6 1986 | |
| OCT 15 1983 | OCT. 27 1986 | |
| MAR. 24 1984 | | |
| OCT. 22 1984 | DEC. 13 1986 | |
| FEB. 28 1985 | SEP. 10 1987 | |

# THIS

## SWEET PICKLES ®

## BOOK BELONGS TO

In the Town of Sweet Pickles, the animals get into and out of pickles because of their all too human personality traits.

Each of the books in the *Sweet Pickles* series is about a different pickle.

This book is about the right time to make jokes ... and the wrong one.

Library of Congress Cataloging in Publication Data

Hefter, Richard.
    Quick Lunch Munch.
    (Sweet Pickles)
    SUMMARY: Kidding Kangaroo, the waiter, is so busy
telling jokes and playing tricks on the diners that no one
gets served at the Quick Lunch Munch Restaurant.
    [1. Kangaroos—Fiction. 2. Restaurants, lunch rooms,
etc.—Fiction]  I. Perle, Ruth Lerner.  II. Title.
PZ7.H3587Qu             [E]              81-7805
ISBN 0-937524-08-5                      AACR2

Published by Euphrosyne, Inc.

Sweet Pickles is the registered trademark of
Perle/Reinach/Hefter

*Printed in the United States of America*

Weekly Reader Books' Edition

**Euphrosyne Incorporated**

Weekly Reader Books Presents

# QUICK LUNCH MUNCH

## Written and Illustrated
## by Richard Hefter
## Edited by Ruth Lerner Perle

It was lunchtime in the Town of Sweet Pickles.
At the restaurant on Center Street, Worried Walrus
was making sure everything was ready for the
noon rush. He came out of the kitchen to check the
dining room.

Kidding Kangaroo, the waiter, was setting the tables. It was his first day on the job.

Walrus stood at the kitchen door and cleared his throat nervously. "Listen, Kangaroo," he said, "I know you've never worked as a waiter before and I'm worried. I'm very worried!"

"Don't worry," smiled Kangaroo. "I'm experienced.
I've waited for a lot of things in my life, so I guess
I can be a good waiter! Haw, haw!"

"That's what I mean," moaned Walrus. "No funny stuff. Just take the orders and serve the food ... as quickly as you can. That's why this restaurant is called the 'Quick Lunch Munch'. People want to have a quick lunch and get going!"

"Don't worry, boss!" giggled Kangaroo. "You keep the food coming and I'll keep the place humming!"

Kangaroo picked up a tray of glasses and kept giggling. He giggléd so hard, the tray began to jiggle. SPLAT! WHOOPS! CRUNCH! The glasses fell off the tray and crashed to the floor.

"Oh, woe!" groaned Walrus. "This is getting to be a problem!"

"Don't worry, boss!" cried Kangaroo. "I was only kidding. I'll get it all cleaned up!"

"I worry. I worry!" sighed Walrus.

Just then, everybody came rushing into the restaurant. Responsible Rabbit and Healthy Hippo were the first to arrive.

Kangaroo handed them some menus. "All right, folks," he said. "What'll it be?"

"I'm in a rush," said Rabbit. "I have to be back at the bank in thirty-one minutes. If I order pancakes, will they be long?"

"No!" laughed Kangaroo. "They'll be round! Haw, haw!"

"I want something warm for lunch," said Hippo. "I see you have soup on the menu."

"Soup on the menu!" chuckled Kangaroo. "I'll give you a clean menu right away!" Kangaroo slapped Hippo on the back and snatched his menu away.

"Oh, dear!" sighed Rabbit. "I came here for lunch, not for jokes!"

"Okay, okay!" grumbled Kangaroo. "I was only kidding. Nobody has a sense of humor any more!"

Nasty Nightingale and Jealous Jackal were sitting at the next table. Nightingale banged on the table with a spoon. "Just a minute, waiter," she yelled. "Do you serve crabs here?"

"Certainly, Madam," chuckled Kangaroo. "We serve anybody. Haw, haw!"

Kangaroo ran off into the kitchen.

"How's it going?" whispered Walrus. "Is everyone being taken care of?"

"Oh, I'm taking care of them, all right!" smiled Kangaroo.

When Kangaroo came back into the dining room, he was carrying a huge tray heaped with plates of food. He gave Rabbit and Hippo their orders.

Hippo looked at his soup. "Just a minute," he said. "There's a fly in my soup!"

"So?" smiled Kangaroo. "How much can a little fly eat? There'll be enough left for you!"

Then Kangaroo put plates in front of Nightingale and Jackal.

"Wait a minute," snarled Jackal. "What is all this stuff? I didn't order this!"

"It's the house special," chuckled Kangaroo. "Strawberry shortcake."

"I hate strawberry shortcake," growled Jackal. "It gives me a rash!"

"Sorry, sir," smiled Kangaroo. "I'll get rid of it." He picked up the strawberry shortcake and tossed it over his shoulder. It landed with a loud PLOP right on Nightingale's head.

"I'll get you for that!" screeched Nightingale. She picked up a hunk of cake and threw it at Kangaroo. Kangaroo ducked and the shortcake sailed right past him. It hit Jackal smack in the face.

BOP! PLOP! WHOOSH! Everybody started throwing shortcakes at each other.

"PHOOEY!" said Kangaroo, pushing strawberry shortcake out of his mouth. "No wonder we can't sell this stuff. It tastes terrible!"

"YAARGHHH!" screamed Nightingale as she threw her last plate. "Now there's nothing left to throw!"

"OH, YES THERE IS!" cried a loud voice. It was Walrus standing at the kitchen door. He was very angry.

"There is something left to throw," moaned Walrus. "I am throwing you all out! You, too, Kangaroo!"